胖打 與 北七熊 日記

Panda & Polar Bear

2

愛 的 悄 悄 話

Panda & Polar Bear 2：Whispers of Love

韋采伶、大衛‧霍金森 著

謹以此書

獻給我們的父親

本書及作者簡介

這是大衛 (Dave Hodgkinson) 與采伶 (Louise Wei) 的半自傳故事，兩個人分別在英國與台灣長大，卻一見鍾情，由於時常在彼此身上感受到不同文化的有趣異同點，於是將這些情節畫成了漫畫，自 2012 年 7 月開始在網路上發表，受到來自世界各地讀者的支持與好評。

官方網站：pandaandpolarbear.com
中文臉書：胖打與北七熊日記
　　　　　PandaAndPolarBearTW

譯 者 簡 介

蘇渝婷（Jill Su)，身兼多職的譯者，熱愛翻譯，迷戀動物，生活無時無刻都環繞著翻譯與動物，就像呼吸般自然。

聯絡方式：a1481a@hotmail.com

周慕姿 《情緒勒索》作者／〈Crescent Lament 恆月三途〉樂團主唱

跟 Louise 的認識，是因為同是台灣少數「歌德金屬」樂團的主唱，兩人「惺惺相惜」，因此即使 Louise 後來在英國定居，我們仍保持聯繫。《胖打與北七熊日記》出了第二集：「愛的悄悄話」。與第一集一樣，這對英倫夫妻的互動，看了仍然令人莞爾一笑。我一直很佩服 Louise 的才華，在她的畫筆下，與 Dave 兩人的互動栩栩如生，躍於紙上；而輕鬆的題材中，隱含伴侶間保持熱情的祕方：在生活的小事中，用欣賞的眼光保持對另一半的好奇。推薦此書，保證療癒！ :）

自 序

轉眼間從台灣來到英國已經八年，從一開始的天真茫然、尋找方向，到後來下定決心努力創作，不知不覺「胖打與北七熊」的漫畫也已累積數百篇了。

還記得兩年前帶著作品返鄉的時候，心裡是多麼地雀躍與驕傲，現在回想起來，只能感恩當初有這份福氣與機會讓父親看到我們的第一本中文書出版。

面對生命的無常，我們只能更加專注的生活在當下，品味每個幸福的時刻，盡力用創作將美好的瞬間留作永恆。

感謝所有親朋好友，也期望「胖打與北七熊」能夠帶給大家無限的快樂與溫暖、寬容和勇氣。

Louise + Dar

※ 為了閱讀方便，本漫畫的中文與英文並非完全對照，是以故事整體的語意通達為準翻譯。

🐾 想像力就是一切
Imagination Is Everything

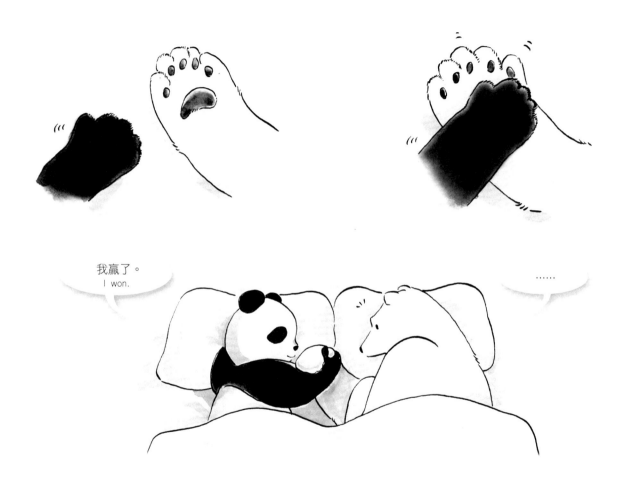

懶熊腕力比賽 🐾
Lazy Arm Wrestling

別動。
Wait.

 BBQ
BBQ

你作夢
Dream On

兩個不能問情侶的尷尬問題 🐾
Two Awkward Questions you DON'T ask Couples

……妳幹嘛？
......WHY?!

是你説「打扮」一下的…
You said "Dress up"...

🐾 **台灣黑胖打**
Formosan Black Panda

你很奇怪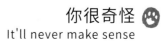
It'll never make sense

Zzzzzz ...

「柏靈頓手忙腳亂的，因為他
正是那種老是給自己惹麻煩的熊……」
"Paddington was in a mess. As he was the
sort of bear who often got himself
into trouble..."

備註：出自邁可‧龐德《柏靈頓熊出國記》。
*From The first paragraph of "Paddington Abroad"
by Michael Bond.

睡前故事
Story Is Us

澎澎的胖打
Panfro

與熊共枕
Unbearable Headache

月亮與你
Moon & You

🐾 末日太妃糖
Toffeegeddon

幫你接話
Finishing Your Sentence For You

1	2	3
準備一杯熱巧克力	豪邁地喝一口	速成鬍子完成！
A cup of hot chocolate	A generous slurp	An instant moustache!

男子漢就是要這樣！
BE A MAN!

🐾 速成鬍子三步驟
Instant Moustache in 3 steps

食蠅熊
Panda Fly Trap

熊貓招喚大法
How To Summon A Panda

我以前也曾經
是那麼的可愛呀！

I used to be that cute!

我的青春小熊一去不回來
On Youth

真相總是殘酷的
The Truth Hurts

胖打電腦難修
IT Panda

啃書的熊
Bookbears

同樣動作，效果有別 🐾
Same Action, Different Effects

新鮮檸檬汁！
Fresh Lemonade!

咕嚕！
Glup!

🐾 一鼓作氣
Glup!

網路上說人要多微笑。
The internet told me to smile more.

網路說了算
The Internet Told Me So

購物趣
On Shopping

她終於要
打掃後院的落葉了！
Finally she's gonna sweep
the dead leaves
in the garden!

掃把
牛奶
麵包
巧克力
啤酒

採買採買…
Doing the groceries,

我真是個好老公！
I'm such a good husband!

這支掃把不管用啊。
This broom is broken.

不管用的掃把
Panda's Broken Broom

我真不敢相信，居然有人會把
這麼多的寶貝丟掉！
I can't believe what people throw away!

我出去丟垃圾喔！
See you in a bit!

不要撿更多東西
回來啦！沒地方放了！
No! We don't have space
for more crap!

胖打最喜歡倒垃圾了，只不過她拿回來的比丟出去的還多⋯
Panda loves doing the trash, it's just she takes more
stuff back in than throws out.

以環保之名
I Can't Believe What People Throw Away

冬眠終結者
The Hibernator

🐾 肚肚太鼓
Belly Taiko

賴在我的肚皮上
Sleeping On Mah Belleh

啊～鬆鬆軟軟的最舒服了！
Ahhh...Nice and foofy!

啊～鬆鬆軟軟的最舒服了！
Ahhh...Nice and foofy!

賴在我的肚皮上 2
Sleeping On Mah Belleh 2

我的雪天使
My Own Snow Angel

胖打麗麗與北七琴
Ukupanda And Cello Bear

教我畫畫吧！
Teach me how to draw!

太棒了！
我可以錄影嗎？
Awesome! Can I video
record it?

不行！
No!

畫畫其實
就像是在表達你自己…
Drawing is a lot like
expressing yourself...

所以要
放開你的感覺…
So just let your
mood flow...

就像這樣？
Like this?

教我畫畫
Teach Me How To Draw

注意月台間隙
Mind The Gap

早上八點
8 a.m.

好大的盲點 🐾
Obviously Whinning

連鎖效應
Chain Fartaction

如同我的履歷所說，
我既風趣又有料，
我很 與眾不同。

As I said on my résumé, I am fun and
interesting, so I suppose
I'm Quirky.

老熊賣瓜
I'm Quirky

十八般武藝樣樣精通，
期待能與您合作！
Skilful Polar Bear
looking forward to work with you!

我很會吃。
I can eat.

求職廣告
Job Ad

不要動啦！
Stop moving !

嗯？
What ?

太好玩了！
嘿嘿，讓我偷偷再動一下下。
This is fun.
I'll move slightly again.

胖打腳架
Pandapod

熊日蝕
Bearclipse

新聞上説
熊貓身上有超強的抗生素…
News says Pandas are good
for antibiotics...

?

寒流來了，
我真的很不想感冒生病…
And I really don't want to
catch a cold & get sick

怎麼啦？
What's wrong?

可是我也不想把她
「吃掉」啊！怎麼辦呢…？
But I don't want to EAT her
either! What to do...?

…這樣也行啦。
......This will do.

增強免疫力，請抱抱胖打
Superhugs For Superbugs

54

啊啊…
Ah...

啊啊…
Ah...

 哈啾
Achoo!!

哎呦！
Ow!

這下變頭痛了。
Now my head hurts.

你什麼都不做，
我怎麼會有新的靈感呢？！
Do something! So I can draw it!

🐾 只看手機的謬思
Do Something

一個愛煮，一個愛吃
One likes to cook, one likes to eat

🐾 煮飯時間
On Cooking

胖打的開飯舞 🐾
Panda Food Dance

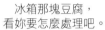
冰箱那塊豆腐，
看妳要怎麼處理吧。
Decide what you want to
do with that Tofu!

好～
OK.

BBC
美味食譜網站
Goodfood

決定了沒？
So?

我決定…要把它吃掉。
I'm gonna EAT IT!

重大的決定
A Big Decision

我不在家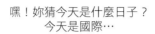
I'm Not Here

62

我在此宣布本日為
I shall declare today as

國際發呆日
The International Day Of Meh

🐾 自行宣布
International Day Of Meh

愛吃鬼的奇幻漂流 🐾
Life Of Pie

一成不變
So Bored

甜蜜的負荷
Happily Occupied

親愛的，我回來啦…
Honey, I am hom....

怕冷的北七熊
Cold Paws Attack

We Got a Cat
in the House

向大家介紹我們家糊塗的新房客：小黑貓！
We've got a new roommate!

🐾 貓咪與水壺
Kitty Versus Kettle

胖打解密
Pandaleaks

北七熊很愛吃辛拉麵喔。

🐾 **火辣之熊**
My Bear Is HOT

筷筷吃飯
Rice Sticks

自由誠可貴
Free Pandas

花粉症
Hey Fever

喵主席
Mao

團隊精神 🐾
I'm A Team Player!

欠揍的攝影師
What Not To Say In Photo Shoot

有時不禁自問
Sometimes We Ask Ourselves

貪杯的主廚
I Like Cooking With Wine

變天如變臉
Unreasonable

創意
How Original

A Typical Day

. . . .

A
Typical
Day

我總是
帶妳去最棒的冒險！
I take you to all the best
adventures.

可是我只想
畫圖啊……！！！
All I wanted...was
to draw...!!!

現在妳就
可以全部畫出來了。
Now you can draw all about it.

……

PANDA
A & PO
LAR 🐾
BEAR

為了新工作，我們準備遷往英國西部的威爾斯，
那是⋯龍的國度！

In search of a new job, the bears are on the move...
to the land of the dragons!

註：本連續插圖為我們向大衛•鮑伊 (David Bowie) 與米克•傑格 (Mick Jagger) 致敬之動畫「在大街跳舞」(Dancing In The Street)，用手機掃 QR code 即可連上 youtube 看影片喔！

釀生活13　PE0095

● ●

Panda & Polar Bear 2 : Whispers of Love

作　者／韋采伶、大衛‧霍金森
翻　譯／蘇渝婷
責任編輯／徐佑驊
圖文排版／蔡瑋筠
封面設計／蔡瑋筠

出版策劃／釀出版
製作發行／秀威資訊科技股份有限公司
114 台北市內湖區瑞光路76巷65號1樓
電話：+886-2-2796-3638
傳真：+886-2-2796-1377
服務信箱：service@showwe.com.tw
http://www.showwe.com.tw

郵政劃撥／19563868
戶名：秀威資訊科技股份有限公司
展售門市／國家書店【松江門市】
104 台北市中山區松江路209號1樓
電話：+886-2-2518-0207
傳真：+886-2-2518-0778

網路訂購／秀威網路書店：http://www.bodbooks.com.tw
　　　　　國家網路書店：http://www.govbooks.com.tw
法律顧問／毛國樑　律師

總經銷／聯合發行股份有限公司
地址：231新北市新店區寶橋路235巷6弄6號4樓
電話：+886-2-2917-8022
傳真：+886-2-2915-6275

出版日期／2017年08月　定價／350元
ISBN／978-986-445-214-9

國家圖書館出版品預行編目

胖打與北七熊日記2：愛的悄悄話 /

　　　　　　韋采伶, 大衛.霍金森作；蘇渝婷翻譯.

-- 臺北市：釀出版, 2017.08

面；　　　　　　　公分. -- (釀生活；13)

BOD版　　　ISBN 978-986-445-214-9(平裝)

855　　　　　　　　　　　106012106

讀者回函卡

感謝您購買本書，為提升服務品質，請填妥以下資料，將讀者回函卡直接寄回或傳真本公司，收到您的寶貴意見後，我們會收藏記錄及檢討，謝謝！

如您需要了解本公司最新出版書目、購書優惠或企劃活動，歡迎您上網查詢或下載相關資料：

http:// www.showwe.com.tw

您購買的書名：_____

出生日期：_____年_____月_____日

學歷：□高中 (含) 以下　　□大專　　□研究所 (含) 以上

職業：□製造業　□金融業　□資訊業　□軍警　□傳播業　□自由業　□服務業　□公務員　□教職
　　　□學生　□家管　□其它_____

購書地點：□網路書店　□實體書店　□書展　□郵購　□贈閱　□其他

您從何得知本書的消息？

　□網路書店　□實體書店　□網路搜尋　□電子報　□書訊　□雜誌　□傳播媒體　□親友推薦

　□網站推薦　□部落格　□其他_____

您對本書的評價：(請填代號　1.非常滿意　2.滿意　3.尚可　4.再改進)

　封面設計_____　版面編排_____　內容_____　文／譯筆_____　價格_____

讀完書後您覺得：

　□很有收穫　□有收穫　□收穫不多　□沒收穫

對我們的建議：_____

_____

_____

_____

11466
台北市內湖區瑞光路 76 巷 65 號 1 樓

秀威資訊科技股份有限公司　　收

BOD 數位出版事業部

⋯⋯⋯⋯⋯⋯⋯⋯⋯⋯⋯⋯⋯⋯⋯⋯⋯⋯⋯⋯⋯⋯⋯⋯⋯⋯⋯⋯⋯⋯⋯⋯⋯⋯

（請沿線對折寄回，謝謝！）

姓　　名：＿＿＿＿＿＿＿＿＿＿＿＿＿　年齡：＿＿＿＿＿　性別：□女　□男

郵遞區號：□□□□□

地　　址：＿＿＿＿＿＿＿＿＿＿＿＿＿＿＿＿＿＿＿＿＿＿＿＿＿＿＿＿＿＿＿

聯絡電話：(日)＿＿＿＿＿＿＿＿＿＿＿＿＿　(夜)＿＿＿＿＿＿＿＿＿＿＿＿＿

E-mail：＿＿＿＿＿＿＿＿＿＿＿＿＿＿＿＿＿＿＿＿＿＿＿＿＿＿＿＿＿＿